It's a sunny summer day in Sunny Town,
with the creatures warm and happy
as the sun shines down.

BUNNIES
ON THE BUS

Philip Ardagh   illustrated by Ben Mantle

CANDLEWICK PRESS

A message to naughty bunnies
everywhere: **BEHAVE!**
P. A.

For the baddest bunny on the block —
Theo Benjamin Wreford-Bush
B. M.

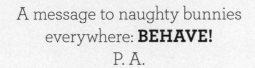

• First U.S. edition 2020 • Library of Congress Catalog Card Number pending • ISBN 978-1-5362-1116-0 • This book was typeset in Archer Book. The illustrations were done in pencil and manipulated digitally. • Candlewick Press, 99 Dover Street, Somerville, Massachusetts 02144 • visit us at www.candlewick.com • Printed in Heshan, Guangdong, China • 20 21 22 23 24 25 LEO 10 9 8 7 6 5 4 3 2 1

There's a turtle at a bus stop
waiting with her shopping.
A bus whizzes past her
with no sign of stopping.

Bunnies on the bus!
Bunnies on the bus!

No wonder there's a fuss
about the bunnies on the bus!

Little Bunny at the wheel!
Little Bunny at the wheel!

He's swerving 'round the corners
to make the others SQUEAL!

Pandas at the crossing!
Pandas at the crossing!

ZOOOOOOOOOOOM!

Their shopping jumping in the air,
spinning and a-tossing.

Bunnies on the bus!
Bunnies on the bus!

No wonder there's a fuss
about the bunnies on the bus!

Baby Bunny wails!
Baby Bunny wails!

Mommy Bunny
SOOTHES him

by reading bunny tales.

Lambs by the library,
playing on the swings.
The bus goes shooting past them,
flying without wings!

Bunnies in the aisle! Bunnies in the aisle!

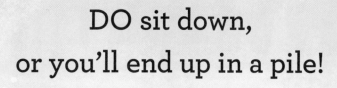

DO sit down,
or you'll end up in a pile!

There's a bunny on the roof! THERE'S A BUNNY ON THE ROOF!

Bunnies on the bus!
Bunnies on the bus!

No wonder there's a fuss
about the bunnies on the bus!

Bunnies at the stop!
Bunnies at the stop!

Time to get off now.

They jump down with a HOP!

But wait.

What's happening
down in Station Lane?

The bunnies from the bus
have jumped onto a . . .

TRAIN!

Bunnies on the train!
Bunnies on the train!

Another bunny journey . . .

Here we go again!